This book
belongs to

This edition published by Parragon Books Ltd in 2014

Parragon Books Ltd
Chartist House
15–17 Trim Street
Bath BA1 1HA, UK
www.parragon.com

ISBN 978-1-4723-6182-0

Printed in China

All About Me

Based on the movie
Once Upon a Princess
written by Craig Gerber
Adapted by Lisa Ann Marsoli
Illustrated by Character Building Studio and the Disney Storybook Artists

Bath · New York · Cologne · Melbourne · Delhi
Hong Kong · Shenzhen · Singapore · Amsterdam

Once upon a time, in the kingdom of Enchancia, there lived a girl called Sofia. She and her mother, Miranda, didn't have much apart from their shoe shop, but they were happy.

One morning, Sofia and her mother went to the castle to give a new pair of shoes to King Roland. It was love at first sight for the king and Miranda.

The couple married and Miranda lovingly greeted the king's children, Princess Amber and Prince James. Then she gave them each a badge she had sewn with their family crest.

King Roland placed a tiara on Sofia's head. "Welcome to the family!"

"I think it's going to take me a while to get the hang of things around here," Sofia said.

Amber nodded. "Just follow my lead and you'll be fine."

Sofia was grateful. Her new sister was going to help her learn everything she needed to know — or so she thought!

At dinner that evening, Sofia counted six different forks by her plate!

King Roland could see it was going to take a while for Sofia to get used to her new royal life. He had a surprise to help her feel welcome. "We will be throwing a royal ball at the end of the week and you and I shall dance the first waltz."

Later on, Sofia went to her mum's room. "I don't know anything about being a princess. And I don't know how to dance."

Miranda smiled down at Sofia and assured her daughter she would be fine if she just tried her best.

Just then, they heard a knock at the door. It was King Roland. He had a beautiful gift for Sofia!

"It's a very special amulet, so you must promise to never take it off. Now, time for bed. You have princess school tomorrow."

Princess school! Sofia liked the sound of that. Maybe she could learn how to act like a real princess in time for the ball after all!

When Amber overheard this, she couldn't help but feel a little jealous of her new sister.

As Sofia skipped back to her room, she bumped into the royal sorcerer, Cedric. His eyes went straight to the amulet around Sofia's neck.

It was the Amulet of Avalor — the powerful charm Cedric had been trying to get for years! With its magic, he could rule over Enchancia himself. Cedric began to think about how he could trick Sofia into giving it to him....

The next morning, Sofia joined Amber and James for the coach ride to Royal Prep Academy. The three headmistresses — Flora, Fauna and Merryweather — greeted her at the gates.

At school, Sofia didn't need to worry about making friends. The other children liked her a lot — which made Amber jealous. She was used to being the popular one!

Amber turned to James. "I think it's time Sofia took a ride on the magic swing."

So James led Sofia to the swing. "Try it! You don't have
to kick. It swings itself."

Sofia climbed onto the swing. She was enjoying the ride
until the swing sped up and sent her flying into the fountain!
Sofia put on a brave smile while the other kids laughed,
but James could tell she was upset. He felt terrible about
tricking his new sister.

Sofia hurried off to dry her dress. Holding back
her tears, she heard frantic chirping coming from
the woods. A baby bird had fallen out of its nest!
She gently placed the tiny bird next to its mother.
As she did, the amulet around her neck began to glow.

When Sofia said goodbye to her new friends
and turned to leave, she thought she heard a tiny,
squeaky voice say, "Thank you". But she must have
been hearing things. Birds didn't talk!

When Sofia arrived home after her awful day at school, Cedric was waiting. "How would you like a private tour of my workshop? Not even the king has seen it!"

In Cedric's workshop, Sofia saw a picture of the Amulet of Avalor. "That looks just like my amulet!"

"But if you had the Amulet of Avalor you would know, because it contains powerful magic. I can take a quick look at it for you?"

But Sofia shook her head.
"I promised to never take it off."
As soon as Cedric saw that his plan wasn't working, he rushed her out of the door. This was going to be tougher than he thought.

The next morning, Sofia awoke to find a surprise on her bed. There was a rabbit called Clover, Whatnaught the squirrel and their bird friends, Robin and Mia. They had come to help her get ready — and Sofia could understand every word they were saying! "I helped a baby bird yesterday and I think the amulet gave me the power to talk to animals."

After breakfast with her new friends, Sofia left for Royal Prep. She hoped her second day would be better!

Although Sofia tried hard in all her classes, she went home feeling sad again. "I thought that being a princess would be easy, but it's really hard."

Miranda had a surprise. She led Sofia to the patio, where her two best friends were waiting at a fancy table set for tea. Sofia was so glad to see them! "Jade! Ruby!"

James joined the party, too. He still felt bad about tricking Sofia and wanted to make it up to her.

Soon Sofia was curtsying and pouring tea like a proper princess, but she told James she still didn't know how to dance.

"No problem. We have dance class with Professor Popov tomorrow. You'll be dancing circles around all of us."

Amber had been watching everyone have fun without her. She had to make sure Sofia didn't dance better than she did.

The next day, before dance class, Amber gave Sofia a sparkling pair of dance slippers to wear.

When Sofia put on the slippers, they took control of her feet. She spun across the floor and then fell into a pile of pillows.

Amber shrugged. "I must have grabbed a pair of Cedric's trick shoes by mistake. Sorry about that."

Sofia decided she couldn't risk another disaster at the ball — princesses just didn't go crashing into things — so when they got home, she went to Cedric for help.

"I have the perfect spell for you." He gave Sofia magic words to say when the waltz began. She didn't know that the spell would put everyone to sleep and help Cedric steal the amulet!

Soon it was time to get ready for the ball. Amber was just admiring herself in the mirror when James came in.

"You gave Sofia the trick shoes on purpose because everyone likes her more than you. And after what you did today, so do I!"

"James! Come back!" Amber quickly rushed after him — and tore her gown! How could she go to the ball now?

Sofia stood in front of her own mirror and stared at herself
in her fancy gown and tiara. She felt like a real princess! For the
first time that week, Sofia was looking forward to the ball!

A little while later, everyone watched as King Roland proudly
escorted a beaming Sofia into the ballroom.

The orchestra began to play. It was time for the first waltz!

Sofia confidently spoke the magic words Cedric had given her: "Somnibus populi cella."

Everyone instantly fell asleep — including Cedric!

"I must have said it wrong!" Sofia ran out of the ballroom. It seemed as if ever since she had become a princess, she couldn't do anything right. Sofia sank to the floor and cried. A tear fell onto her amulet and suddenly, Cinderella appeared!

"Your amulet brought me here. It links all the princesses that ever were and when one of us is in trouble, another will come to help. Why are you so sad, Sofia?"

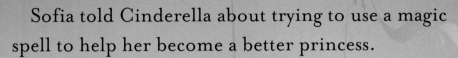

Sofia told Cinderella about trying to use a magic spell to help her become a better princess.

Cinderella smiled and then she explained that she wasn't always a princess, either. But she discovered that the people who truly cared about you didn't care which fork you used or how well you danced.

Cinderella couldn't undo the spell, but she suggested that Sofia try to become true sisters with Amber — something she had never been able to do with her own stepsisters. "Perhaps all she needs is a second chance." Then Cinderella disappeared!

Sofia went to Amber's room. "I've done something terrible."
She told Amber about the spell and then led her to the ballroom.
Sofia felt terrible. "It's all my fault."
Amber shook her head. "No, Sofia. You wouldn't have needed
the spell if I hadn't given you those trick shoes."
The girls realized that what they really needed was each other.

Together they went to Cedric's workshop to find a counterspell to wake everyone up. Clover, Whatnaught, Mia and Robin helped to lock Cedric's pet raven, Wormwood, in his cage.

Wormwood didn't realize that with her amulet, Sofia could understand every word he said. So Clover tricked him into revealing where the counterspell book was hidden.

Now Cedric's spell could be broken!

Sofia and Amber were rushing to the ballroom when Amber remembered her torn dress. "I can't go in looking like this."

But Sofia wasn't about to leave her sister behind, so she quickly mended the gown. "There you go. Good as new!"

Now it was Amber's turn to help. She led her sister in a waltz until Sofia was ready for the ball.

Sofia smiled as she took her place beside the king. Then she said, "Populi cella excitate!" To her relief, everyone woke up.

Cedric was furious that his plan had been ruined!
"Merlin's mushrooms!" he muttered and flicked his wand
and disappeared in a puff of smoke.

Meanwhile, Sofia and the king began to waltz.

Sofia looked up at her new dad. "I've been wondering. Why do they call you Roland the Second?"

The king explained to Sofia that his father had also been named Roland.

"So I guess that makes me Sofia the First," Sofia said.

And it was plain to see that this princess was going to live happily ever after!

The End

Meet Sofia

This is Sofia.

Can you wave hello to her?

Let's be friends!

Sofia loves to make new friends.
Would you like to be Sofia's friend?

Friends tell each other all about who they are.

Sofia is eight years old.
How old are you?

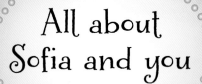

All about Sofia and you

Let's discover more about Sofia and you!

Sofia has reddish-brown hair.
What colour is your hair?

Sofia has blue eyes.
What colour are your eyes?

Smile for Sofia!

Sofia wants to see what you look like! In the box below, draw or stick in a picture of you smiling.

Sofia's parents

Sofia is a princess!

Her mother married King Roland and she is now Queen Miranda!

Can you draw a big heart around the king and queen?

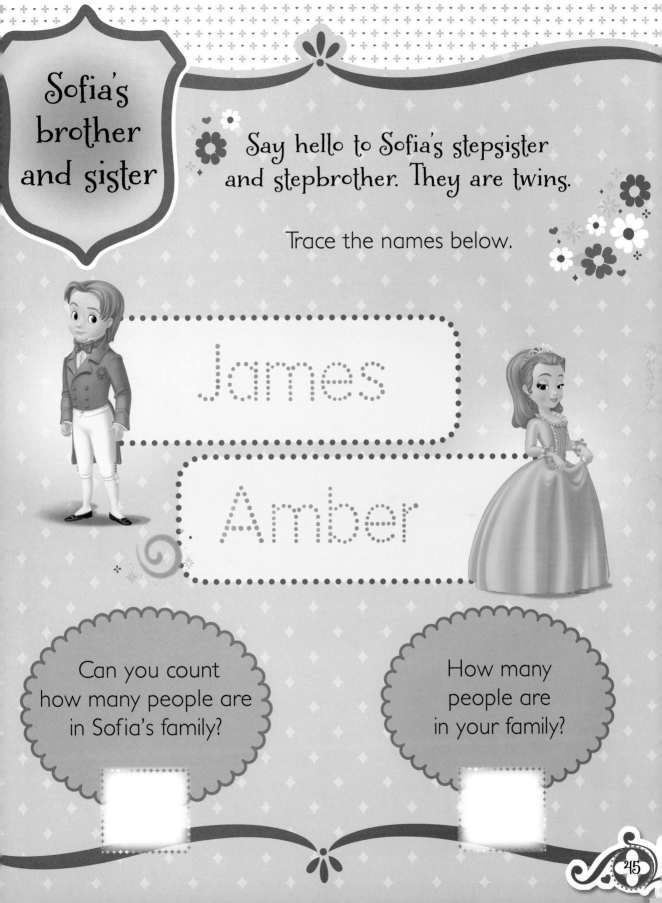

Sofia's brother and sister

Say hello to Sofia's stepsister and stepbrother. They are twins.

Trace the names below.

James

Amber

Can you count how many people are in Sofia's family?

How many people are in your family?

Your family

It's time for Sofia to meet your family!

Draw or stick in a family photo here.

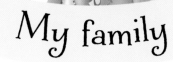

My family

_____ is my _____

_____ is my _____

_____ is my _____

_____ is my _____

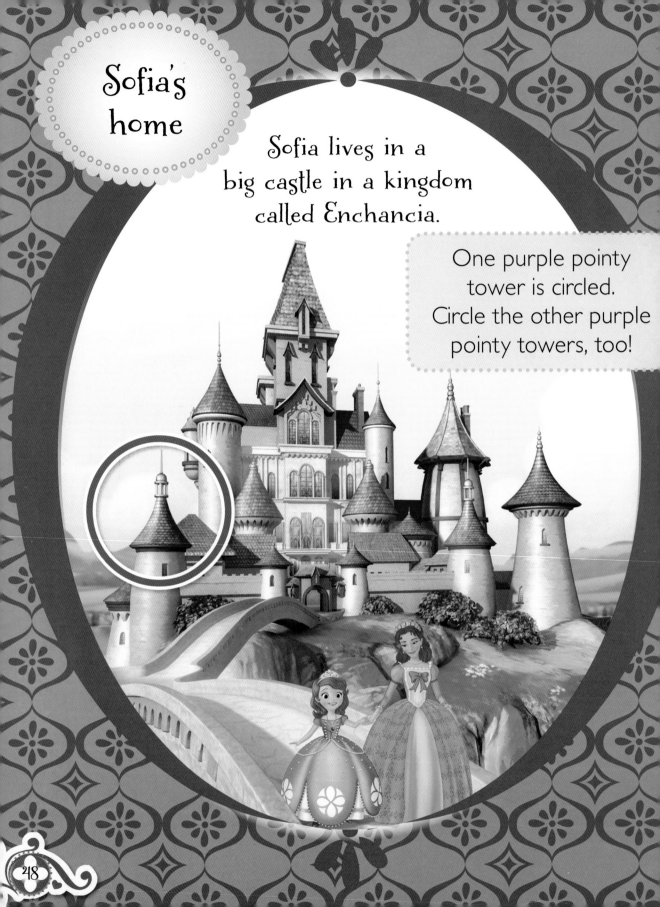

Sofia's home

Sofia lives in a big castle in a kingdom called Enchancia.

One purple pointy tower is circled. Circle the other purple pointy towers, too!

Your home

I live in a place called

Tell Sofia about where you live.

Draw your house or stick in a photo of it here.

Sofia's room

This is where Sofia sleeps, does her homework and plays with her friends.

How many pillows does Sofia have?

Your room

Now draw your room, so that Sofia can see what it looks like.

Dress-up time for Sofia ...

So many grand balls are held in the castle! Sofia is getting ready for one right now.

Help Sofia by colouring in her gown.

and for you, too!

Sofia wants you to go with her to the ball!

Point to the things you would wear.

So much to learn!

Sofia is learning lots of new things at her school, Royal Prep.

Tick the things you would like to learn in school.

$2+2=4$

Maths

Reading

Gardening

Horse riding

Painting

Making tea

Sofia's amulet

King Roland gave Sofia
a beautiful amulet. It allows her
to understand animals!

Draw a line between each animal
and the sound it makes.

Neigh

Squeak

Tweet, tweet

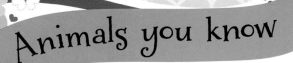

Animals you know

Do you or any of your
friends have a pet?

Draw or stick in a picture of an animal you
would like to have as a pet and give it a name.

Say hello to

Meet Sofia's animal friends

Sofia has some very special friends.

Use the words below to help you write down what kind of animal each one is.

Rabbit

Bluebird

Robin

Squirrel

Clover

Clover is Sofia's best animal friend. He has a big heart and is always hungry!

Clover is a

Mia is very pretty. She sings sweetly and is very kind.

Mia is a

Mia

Whatnaught is usually with Clover. He doesn't talk, but he smiles a lot!

Whatnaught is a

Whatnaught

Robin is very clever. She looks out for the other animals and makes sure they are okay.

Robin is a

Robin